1995

D0467205

Binya's Blue Umbrella

Binya's Blue Umbrella

□ BY *Ruskin Bond* □
ILLUSTRATED BY Vera Rosenberry

BOYDS MILLS PRESS

Text copyright © 1995 by Ruskin Bond
Illustrations copyright © 1995 by Vera Rosenberry
All rights reserved

Published by Caroline House
Boyds Mills Press, Inc.
A Highlights Company
815 Church Street
Honesdale, Pennsylvania 18431
Printed in the United States of America

Publisher Cataloging-in-Publication Data
Bond, Ruskin.
Binya's blue umbrella / by Ruskin Bond ; illustrated by
Vera Rosenberry.—1st ed.
[72]p. : ill. ; cm.
Summary : Binya, a young girl living in rural India, trades her leopard-
claw necklace for a dainty blue umbrella, but the local tea shop proprietor
wants the umbrella for his own.
ISBN 1-56397-135-6
1. India—Juvenile fiction. [1. India—Fiction.]
I. Rosenberry, Vera, ill. II. Title.
813'.54 [F]—dc20   1995   CIP
Library of Congress Catalog Card Number 94-71026

First edition, 1995
Book designed by Jean Krulis
The text of this book is set in 14-point Garamond Light.
Distributed by St. Martin's Press

10 9 8 7 6 5 4 3 2 1

For Siddharth—
good luck, little one.
—R. B.

To Rajalakshmi
—V. R.

Binya's Blue Umbrella

□ CHAPTER ONE □

"Neelu! Neelu!" cried Binya. She scrambled barefoot over the rocks, ran over the short summer grass, up and over the brow of the hill, all the time calling "Neelu, Neelu!"

Neelu—Blue—was the name of the blue-gray cow. The other cow, which was white, was called Gori, meaning Fair One. They were fond of wandering off on their own, down to the stream or into the pine forest,

9

and sometimes they stayed away—almost deliberately, it seemed to Binya.

If the cows didn't come home at the right time, Binya would be sent to fetch them. Sometimes her brother, Bijju, went with her, but these days he was busy preparing for his exams and didn't have time to help with the cows.

Binya liked being on her own, and sometimes she allowed the cows to lead her into some distant valley. Then they would all be late coming home. The cows preferred having Binya with them because she let them wander. Bijju pulled them by their tails if they went too far.

Binya lived in the small village of Tibri in the western Himalayas at a height of seven thousand feet above sea level. Here there were five seasons: winter, when cold winds swept down from the higher peaks, bringing sleet and snow; spring, when the apple and peach blossoms covered the lower slopes; a brief, hot summer, when the mountain grass turned brown and yellow; a three-month-long monsoon season of almost incessant rain, when lush green foliage sprang up everywhere; then a brief, golden autumn of soft breezes and cloudless blue skies.

It was late June now, time for the monsoon to arrive. The days were long, the sun bathing the hills in golden light till about seven in the evening.

Binya belonged to the mountains, to this part of the Himalayas known as Garhwal. Dark forests and lonely hilltops held no terrors for Binya. It was only when she was in the marketplace of a nearby town, jostled by the crowds in the bazaar, that she felt rather nervous and lost. The town, seven miles from the village, was a pleasure resort for tourists from all over India.

Binya was probably ten. She may have been nine or even eleven; she couldn't be sure because no one in the village kept birthdays. Her mother told her she'd been born during the winter when the snow had come up to the windows, and that was just over ten years ago, wasn't it? Two years later her father had died, but his passing had made no difference to their way of life. They had three tiny terraced fields on the side of the mountain, and they grew potatoes, onions, ginger, beans, mustard, and maize—not enough to sell in the town, but enough to live on.

Like most mountain girls, Binya was quite sturdy. She had fair skin with pink cheeks and dark eyes, and her black hair was tied in a ponytail. She wore pretty glass bangles on her wrists and a necklace of blue and yellow agate. From the necklace hung a leopard's claw—a lucky charm—and Binya always wore it. Bijju had one, too, only his was attached to a string.

Binya's full name was Binyadevi, and Bijju's real name was Vijay, but everyone called them Binya and Bijju. Binya was about two years younger than her brother.

Binya had stopped calling for Neelu. She heard the cowbells tinkling and knew the cow hadn't gone far. Singing to herself, Binya walked over fallen pine needles into the forest glade on the spur of the hill. She heard voices, laughter, the clatter of plates and cups. Stepping through the trees, she came upon a party of picnickers.

They were holiday-makers from the plains. The women were dressed in bright saris, the men wore light summer shirts, and the children had pretty new clothes. Binya, standing in the shadows between the trees, went unnoticed. For some time she watched the picnickers, admiring their clothes, listening to their unfamiliar accents, and gazing rather hungrily at the sight of all their food. And then her gaze came to rest on a bright blue umbrella, a frilly thing for women, which lay open on the grass beside its owner.

Now Binya had seen umbrellas before. Her mother had a big black umbrella that nobody used anymore because the field rats had eaten holes in it. But this was the first time Binya had seen such a small, dainty, colorful umbrella—and she fell in love with it. The umbrella was like a flower, a great blue flower that had sprung up on the dry brown hillside.

She moved forward a few paces so that

she could see the umbrella better. As she came out of the shadows into the sunlight, the picnickers saw her.

"Hello, look who's here!" exclaimed the older of the two women. "A little village girl!"

"Isn't she pretty?" remarked the other. "But how torn and dirty her clothes are!" It did not seem to bother them that Binya could hear and understand everything they said about her.

"They're very poor in the hills," said one of the men.

"Then let's give her something to eat." And the older woman beckoned to Binya to come closer.

Hesitantly, nervously, Binya approached the group. Normally she would have turned and fled, but her attraction to the pretty blue umbrella made her bold. It had cast a spell over her, drawing her forward almost against her will.

"What's that on her neck?" asked the younger woman.

"A necklace of sorts."

"It's a pendant—see, there's a claw hanging from it!"

"It's a tiger's claw," said the man beside her. (He had never seen a tiger's claw.) "A lucky charm. These people wear them to keep away evil spirits." He looked to Binya for confirmation, but Binya said nothing.

"Oh, I want one, too!" said the woman, who was obviously his wife.

"You can't get them in shops."

"Buy hers, then. Give her two or three rupees. She's sure to need the money."

The man, looking slightly embarrassed but anxious to please his young wife, produced a two-rupee note and offered it to Binya, indicating that he wanted the pendant in exchange. Binya put her hand to the necklace, half afraid that the excited woman would snatch it away from her. Solemnly she shook her head. The man then showed her a five-rupee note, but again Binya shook her head.

"How silly she is!" exclaimed the young woman.

"It may not be hers to sell," said the

man. "But I'll try again. How much do you want—what can we give you?" And he waved his hand toward the picnic things scattered about on the grass.

Without any hesitation Binya pointed to the umbrella.

"My umbrella!" exclaimed the young woman. "She wants my umbrella. What cheek!"

"Well, you want her pendant, don't you?"

"That's different."

"Is it?"

The man and his wife were beginning to quarrel with each other.

"I'll ask her to go away," said the older woman. "We're making such fools of ourselves."

"But I *want* the pendant!" cried the other petulantly. And then, on an impulse, she picked up the umbrella and held it out to Binya. "Here, take the umbrella!"

Binya removed her necklace and held it out to the young woman, who immediately placed it around her own neck. Then Binya took the umbrella and held it up. It did not look so small in her hands; in fact, it was just the right size.

She had forgotten about the picnickers, who were busy examining the pendant. She turned the blue umbrella this way and that, looking through the bright blue silk at the pulsating sun. Then, still keeping it open, she turned and disappeared into the forest glade.

□ CHAPTER TWO □

Binya seldom closed the blue umbrella. Even when she had it in the house, she left it lying open in a corner of the room. Sometimes Bijju snapped it shut, complaining that it got in the way. She would open it again a little later. It wasn't beautiful when it was closed.

Whenever Binya went out—whether it was to graze the cows, or fetch water from the spring, or carry milk to the little tea shop on the Tehri road—she took the umbrella with her. That patch of sky-blue silk could always be seen on the hillside.

Although Binya had plenty to do, most of the work in and around the home was done by Binya's mother. Like most hill women, she was sturdy, handsome rather than pretty, strong in the forearms from cutting wood or grass and tilling their small field, strong in the legs from climbing the steep paths that zigzagged up and down the steep hillsides.

She could climb trees, too. She was better at this than Bijju, who usually fell out of trees. When the rhododendron trees were in bloom, their mother collected the scarlet blossoms from the tops of the trees. They were made into a jam or chutney. Rhododendron jam was a favorite of Bijju's, although Binya preferred the apricot jam that her mother made in early summer.

With their mother's help, they also grew potatoes, beans, and cucumbers. And when they had a surplus of vegetables they exchanged them for rice or flour in the nearby town.

Old Ram Bharosa (Ram the Trustworthy) kept the tea shop on the Tehri road. It was a dusty, unmetalled road. Once a day the Tehri bus stopped near the shop, and passengers got down to sip hot tea or drink a glass of curds. He kept a few bottles of cola, too; but as there was no ice, the bottles got hot in the sun and were seldom opened. He also kept sweets and toffees, and when Binya or Bijju had a few coins to spare, they would spend them at the shop. It was only a mile from the village.

Ram Bharosa was astonished to see Binya's blue umbrella.

"What have you got there, Binya?" he asked.

Binya gave the umbrella a twirl and smiled at Ram Bharosa. She was always ready with her smile and would willingly have shown it to anyone who was feeling unhappy.

"That's a lady's umbrella," said Ram

Bharosa. "That's only for memsahibs. Where did you get it?"

"Someone gave it to me—for my necklace."

"You exchanged it for your lucky claw!"

Binya nodded.

"But what do you need it for? The sun isn't hot enough—and it isn't meant for the rain. It's just a pretty thing for rich ladies to play with!"

Binya nodded and smiled again. Ram Bharosa was quite right. It was just a beautiful plaything, and that was exactly why she had fallen in love with it.

"I have an idea," said the shopkeeper. "It's no use to you, that umbrella. Why not sell it to me? I'll give you five rupees for it."

"It's worth fifteen," said Binya.

"Well, then I'll give you ten."

Binya laughed and shook her head.

"Twelve rupees?" said Ram Bharosa, but without much hope.

Binya placed a five-paise coin on the counter. "I came for a toffee," she said.

Ram Bharosa pulled at his drooping

whiskers, gave Binya a wry look, and placed a toffee in the palm of her hand. He watched Binya as she walked away along the dusty road. The blue umbrella held him fascinated, and he stared after it until it was out of sight.

□ CHAPTER THREE □

The villagers used the same road to go to the market town. Some went by bus, a few rode on mules, but most people walked. Today, everyone on the road turned to stare at the girl with the bright blue umbrella.

Binya sat down in the shade of a pine tree. The umbrella, still open, lay beside her. She cradled her head in her arms and presently dozed off. It was that kind of day, sleepy warm and summery.

And while she slept, a wind sprang up.

It came quietly, swishing gently through the trees, humming softly. Then it was joined by other random gusts bustling over the tops of the mountains. The trees shook their heads and came to life. The wind fanned Binya's cheeks. The umbrella stirred on the grass.

The wind grew stronger, picking up dead leaves and sending them spinning and swirling through the air. It got into the umbrella and began to drag it over the grass. Suddenly it lifted the umbrella and carried it about six feet from the sleeping girl. The sound woke Binya.

She was on her feet immediately, and then she was leaping down the steep slope. But just as she was within reach of the umbrella, the wind picked it up again and carried it farther downhill.

Binya set off in pursuit. The wind was in a wicked, playful mood. It would leave the umbrella alone for a few moments, but as soon as Binya came near, it would pick up the umbrella again and send it bouncing, floating, dancing away from her.

The hill grew steeper. Binya knew that after twenty yards it would fall away in a precipice. She ran faster. The wind ran with her, ahead of her, and the blue umbrella stayed up with the wind.

A fresh gust picked it up and carried it to the very edge of the cliff. There it balanced for a few seconds before toppling over, out of sight.

Binya ran to the edge of the cliff. Going down on her hands and knees, she peered down the cliff-face. About a hundred feet below, a small stream rushed between great boulders. Hardly anything grew on the cliff-face—just a few stunted bushes and, halfway down, a wild cherry tree growing crookedly out of the rocks and hanging across the chasm. The umbrella had stuck in the cherry tree.

Binya didn't hesitate. She may have been timid with strangers, but she was at home on a hillside. She stuck her bare leg over the edge of the cliff and began climbing. Binya kept her face to the hillside, feeling the way with her feet, only changing her handhold when she knew her feet were secure. Sometimes she held on to the thorny bilberry bushes, but she did not trust the other plants, which came away very easily.

Loose stones rattled down the cliff. Once on their way, the stones did not stop until they reached the bottom of the hill. They took other stones with them, so that soon there was a cascade of stones, and Binya had to be very careful not to start a landslide.

As agile as a mountain goat, she did not take more than five minutes to reach the crooked cherry tree. But the most difficult task remained. She had to crawl along the trunk of the tree, which stood out at a right angle from the cliff. Only by doing this could she reach the trapped umbrella.

Binya felt no fear when climbing trees. She was proud of the fact that she could climb as well as Bijju. Gripping the rough cherry bark with her toes and using her

knees as leverage, she crawled along the trunk of the projecting tree until she was almost within reach of the umbrella. She noticed with dismay that the blue cloth was torn in a couple of places.

She looked down, and it was only then that she felt afraid. She was right over the chasm, balanced precariously about eighty feet above the boulder-strewn stream. Looking down, she felt quite dizzy. Her hands shook, and the tree shook, too. If she slipped now, there was only one direction in which she could fall—down, down, into the depths of that dark and shadowy ravine.

There was only one thing to do: concentrate on the patch of blue just a couple of feet away from her.

She did not look down or up, but straight ahead. Willing herself forward, she managed to reach the umbrella.

She could not crawl back with it in her hands. So, after dislodging it from the forked branch in which it had stuck, she let it fall, still open, into the ravine below. Cushioned by the wind, the umbrella floated serenely downward, landing in a thicket of nettles.

Binya crawled back along the trunk of the cherry tree.

Twenty minutes later she emerged from the nettle clump, her precious umbrella held aloft. She had nettle stings all over her legs, but she was hardly aware of the smarting. She'd feel them later, when she got home.

□ CHAPTER FOUR □

Next day, Bijju was on his way home from school. It was two o'clock, and he hadn't eaten since six in the morning. Fortunately, the Kingora bushes—the bilberries—were in fruit, and Bijju's lips were already stained purple with the juice of the wild, sour fruit. He didn't have any money to spend at Ram Bharosa's shop, but he stopped anyway to look at the sweets in their glass jars.

"And what will you have today?" asked Ram Bharosa.

"No money," said Bijju.

"You can pay me later."

Bijju shook his head. Some of his friends had taken sweets on credit, and at the end of the month they had found they'd eaten more sweets than they could possibly pay for! As a result, they'd had to hand over to Ram Bharosa some of their most treasured possessions—a curved knife for cutting grass, a small hand ax, a jar for pickles, or a pair of earrings. These had become the shopkeeper's property and were kept by him or sold in his shop. It was more than just a simple tea shop. Anything that could be resold at a small profit found its way there.

Ram Bharosa had set his heart on having Binya's blue umbrella, and so naturally he was anxious to give credit to either of the children. But so far neither had fallen into the trap.

Bijju moved on, his mouth full of Kingora berries. Halfway home, he saw Binya with

the cows. It was getting late, and the sun was going down, but Binya still had the umbrella open. The two small rents had been stitched up by their mother.

Bijju gave his sister a handful of berries. She handed him the umbrella while she ate the berries.

"You can have the umbrella until we get home," she said. It was her way of thanking Bijju for bringing her the wild fruit.

Calling "Neelu! Gori!" Binya and Bijju set out for home, followed at some distance by the cows.

It was dark before they reached the village, but they still had the umbrella open.

□ CHAPTER FIVE □

Most of the people in the village were a little envious of Binya's blue umbrella. No one else had ever possessed one like it. The schoolmaster's wife thought it was quite wrong for a poor farmer's daughter to have such a fine umbrella while she, a second-class college graduate, had to make do with an ordinary black one. When her husband offered to have their old umbrella dyed blue, she gave him a scornful look and loved him a little less than before. The village priest, who looked after the temple, announced that he would buy a multicolored umbrella the next time he was in the town. A few days later he returned, looking annoyed and grumbling that they weren't available except in Delhi. Most people consoled themselves by saying that Binya's pretty umbrella wouldn't keep out the rain if it rained heavily, that it would shrivel in the sun if the sun was fierce, that it would collapse in the wind if the wind was strong, that it would attract lightning if lightning fell near it, and that it would prove unlucky if there was any ill-luck going about. Secretly, everyone admired it.

Unlike the adults, the children didn't have to pretend. They were full of praise for the umbrella. It was so light, so pretty, so bright a blue! And it was just the right size for Binya. They knew that if they said nice things about the umbrella, Binya would smile and give it to them to hold for a little while—just a very little while!

Soon it was the time of the monsoon.

Big black clouds kept piling up, and thunder rolled over the hills.

Binya sat on the hillside all afternoon, waiting for the rain. As soon as the first big drop of rain came down, she raised the umbrella over her head. More drops, big ones, came pattering down. She could see them through the umbrella silk as they broke against the cloth.

And then there was a cloudburst, and it was like standing under a waterfall. The umbrella wasn't really a rain umbrella, but it held up bravely. Only Binya's feet got wet. Rods of rain fell around her in a curtain of slivered glass.

Everywhere on the hillside people were scurrying for shelter. Some made for a charcoal-burner's hut; others for a mule shed, or Ram Bharosa's shop. Binya was the only one who didn't run. This was what she'd been waiting for—rain on her umbrella—and she wasn't in a hurry to go home. She didn't mind getting her feet wet. The cows didn't mind getting wet either.

Presently she found Bijju sheltering in a

cave. He would have enjoyed getting wet, but he had school books with him and couldn't afford to let them get spoiled. When he saw Binya, he came out of the cave and shared the umbrella. He was a head taller than his sister, so he had to hold the umbrella for her while she held his books.

The cows had been left far behind.

"Neelu, Neelu!" called Binya.

"Gori!" called Bijju.

When their mother saw them sauntering home through the driving rain, she called out, "Binya! Bijju! Hurry up, and bring the cows in! What are you doing there in the rain?"

"Just testing the umbrella," said Bijju.

□ CHAPTER SIX □

The rains set in, and the sun made only brief appearances. The hills turned a lush green. Ferns sprang up on walls and tree trunks. Giant lilies reared up like leopards from the tall grass. A white mist coiled and uncoiled as it floated up from the valley. It was a beautiful season, except for the leeches.

Every day, Binya came home with a couple of leeches fastened to the flesh of her bare legs. The leeches fell off by themselves just as soon as they'd had their thimbleful of blood. You didn't know they were on you until they fell off; and then, later, your skin became very sore and itchy. Some of the older people still believed that being bled by leeches was a remedy for various ailments. Whenever Ram Bharosa had a headache, he applied a leech to his throbbing temple.

Three days of incessant rain had flooded out a number of small animals who lived in holes in the ground. Binya's mother suddenly found the roof crawling with field rats. She had to drive them out; they ate too much of her stored-up wheat flour and rice. Bijju liked to lift large rocks, thus disturbing the scorpions who were sleeping beneath. And snakes came out to bask in the sun.

Binya had just crossed the small stream at the bottom of the hill when she saw something gliding out of the bushes and coming toward her. It was a long black snake. A clatter of loose stones frightened

it. Seeing the girl in its way, it rose up, hissing, and prepared to strike. The forked tongue darted out, and the venomous head lunged at Binya.

Binya's umbrella was open as usual. She thrust it forward between herself and the snake. The snake's hard snout thudded twice against the strong silk of the umbrella. The reptile then turned and slithered away over the wet rocks, disappearing in a clump of ferns.

Binya forgot about the cows and ran all the way home to tell her mother how she had been saved by the umbrella. Bijju had to put away his books and go out to fetch the cows. He carried a stout stick in case he met with any snakes.

□ CHAPTER SEVEN □

First the summer sun and now the endless rain meant that the umbrella was beginning to fade a little. From a bright blue it had changed to a light blue. But it was still a pretty thing, and tougher than it looked. Ram Bharosa still desired it. He did not want to sell it; he wanted to own it. He was probably the richest man in the area—so why shouldn't he have a blue umbrella? Not a day passed without his getting a glimpse of Binya and the umbrella; and the more he saw the umbrella, the more he wanted it.

The schools closed during the monsoon, but this didn't mean that Bijju could sit at home doing nothing. Neelu and Gori were providing more milk than was required at home, so Binya's mother was able to sell a kilo of milk every day: half a kilo to the schoolmaster and half a kilo (at a reduced rate) to the temple priest. Bijju had to deliver the milk every morning.

Ram Bharosa had asked Bijju to work in his shop during the holidays, but Bijju didn't have time. He had to help his mother with the ploughing and the trans-plantation of the rice seedlings. So Ram Bharosa employed a boy from the next village, a boy called Rajaram. He did all the washing-up and ran various errands. He went to the same school as Bijju, but the two were not friends.

One day, as Binya passed the shop, twirling her blue umbrella, Rajaram noticed that his employer gave a deep sigh and began muttering to himself.

"What's the matter, babuji?" asked the boy. He was always careful to use the respectful term babuji, or sir.

"Oh, nothing," said Ram Bharosa. "It's just a sickness that has come upon me. And it's all due to that girl, Binya."

"Why, what has she done to you?"

"Refused to sell me her umbrella! There's pride for you. And I offered her ten rupees."

"Perhaps, if you gave her twelve . . ."

"But it isn't new any longer. It isn't worth eight rupees now. All the same, I'd like to have it."

"You wouldn't make a profit on it," said Rajaram.

"It's not the profit I'm after, wretch! It's the thing itself. It's the beauty of it!"

"And what would you do with it, babuji? You don't visit anyone—you're seldom out of your shop. Of what use would it be to you?"

"Of what use is a poppy in a cornfield?

Of what use is a rainbow? Of what use are you, numbskull? Wretch! I, too, have a soul. I want the umbrella because—because I want its beauty to be mine!"

Rajaram put the kettle on to boil and began dusting the counter, all the time muttering, "I'm as useful as an umbrella." Then, after a short period of intense thought, he said, "What will you give me, babuji, if I get the umbrella for you?"

"What do you mean?" asked the old man.

"A small reward, babuji?"

"You mean to steal it, don't you, you wretch? What a delightful child you are! I'm glad you're not my son or my enemy. But, look—everyone will know it has been stolen, and then how will I be able to show off with it?"

"You will have to look upon it in secret," said Rajaram with a chuckle. "Or take it into Tehri town and have it dyed red! But tell me, babuji, do you want it badly enough to pay me five rupees for removing it without being seen?"

Ram Bharosa gave the boy a long, sad

look. "You're a sharp boy," he said. "You'll come to a bad end. I'll give you two rupees."

"Five," said Rajaram.

"Three," said Ram Bharosa.

"You don't really want it, I can see that," said the boy.

"Wretch!" said the old man. "Evil one! Darkener of my doorstep! Fetch me the umbrella, and I'll give you five rupees!"

□ CHAPTER EIGHT □

A few days later, Binya was in the forest glade where she had first seen the umbrella. No one came there for picnics during the monsoon. The grass was always wet, and the pine needles were slippery underfoot. The tall trees shut out the light, and strange-looking mushrooms, orange and purple, sprang up everywhere. But it was a good place for porcupines, who seemed to like the mushrooms, and Binya was searching for porcupine quills.

Hill people didn't think much of porcupine quills, but far away in southern India the quills were valued as charms and sold at a rupee each. So Ram Bharosa paid a tenth of a rupee for each quill brought to him, and he in turn sold the quills at a profit to a trader from the plains.

Binya had already found five quills, and she knew there'd be more in the long grass. For once, she'd put her umbrella down. She had to put it aside if she wanted to search the ground thoroughly.

It was Rajaram's chance.

The boy had been following Binya for some time, concealing himself behind trees and rocks, creeping closer whenever she became absorbed in her search. He was anxious that she should not see him and be able to recognize him later.

He waited until Binya had wandered some distance from the umbrella. Then, running forward at a crouch, he seized the open umbrella and dashed off with it.

But Rajaram had very big feet. Binya heard his heavy footsteps and turned just in time to see him as he disappeared between the trees. She cried out, dropped the porcupine quills, and gave chase.

Binya was swift and surefooted, but Rajaram had a long stride. All the same, he made the mistake of running downhill. A long-legged person is much faster going uphill than down. Binya reached the edge of the forest glade in time to see the thief scrambling down the path to the stream. He had closed the umbrella so that it would not hinder his flight.

Binya was beginning to gain on the boy. He kept to the path, while she simply slid and leapt down the steep hillside. Near the bottom of the hill the path began to straighten out, and it was here that the long-legged boy began to forge ahead again.

Bijju was coming home from another direction. He had a bundle of sticks that he'd collected for the kitchen fire. As he reached the path, he saw Binya rushing down the hill as though all the mountain spirits were after her.

"What's wrong?" he called. "Why are you running?"

Binya paused only to point at the fleeing Rajaram.

"My umbrella!" she cried. "He has stolen it!"

Bijju dropped his bundle of sticks and ran after his sister. When he reached her side, he said, "I'll soon catch him!" and went sprinting away over the lush green grass. He was fresh, and was soon well ahead of Binya and gaining on the thief.

Rajaram was crossing the shallow stream when Bijju caught up with him. Rajaram was the taller boy, but Bijju was much stronger. He flung himself at the thief, caught him by the legs, and brought him down in the water. Rajaram got to his feet and tried to drag himself away, but Bijju still had him by a leg. Rajaram over-balanced and came down with a great splash. He let the umbrella fall, and it

began to float away on the current. Just then Binya arrived, flushed and breathless, and went dashing into the stream after the umbrella.

Meanwhile, a tremendous fight was taking place. Locked in fierce combat, the two boys swayed together on a rock, tumbled onto the sand, and rolled over and over the pebbled bank until they were again thrashing about in the stream. The magpies, bulbuls, and other birds were disturbed, and they flew away with cries of alarm.

Covered with mud, gasping and spluttering, the boys groped for each other in the water. After five minutes of frenzied struggle, Bijju emerged victorious. Rajaram lay flat on his back on the sand, exhausted, while Bijju sat astride him, pinning him down with his arms and legs.

"Let me get up!" gasped Rajaram. "Let me go—I don't want your useless umbrella!"

"Then why did you take it?" demanded Bijju. "Come on—tell me why!"

"It was that skinflint, Ram Bharosa," said

Rajaram. "He told me to get it for him. He said if I didn't fetch it, I'd lose my job."

"I don't believe you," said Bijju. But he let him get up. He knew they would have no further trouble with Rajaram, now that he'd been confronted with the theft. Rajaram valued his skin more than Ram Bharosa's coins.

□ CHAPTER NINE □

By early October the rains were coming to an end. The leeches disappeared. The ferns turned yellow, and the sunlight on the green hills was mellow and golden like the leaves of the small walnut tree in front of Binya's home.

Binya's mother returned from their field, her arms laden with ripe corncobs. Roasted and salted, they were Bijju's favorite snack.

The front courtyard was ablaze with red

chilies spread out on a mat to dry. In the middle of the chilies sat a large yellow pumpkin and a few fresh limes. Binya sat on the steps of the house, slowly and methodically knitting a pullover for her mother. Her mother didn't get time for knitting.

Bijju's days were happy ones. He would walk slowly home from school, munching on roasted corn. Binya's umbrella had turned a pale milky blue and was patched in several places, but it was still the prettiest umbrella in the village, and she still carried it with her wherever she went.

The cold, cruel winter wasn't far off. But somehow October seemed longer than other months because it was a kind month: the grass was good to lie upon, the breeze was warm and gentle and pine-scented. That October everyone seemed contented— everyone, that is, except Ram Bharosa.

He grumbled at everything, including the glorious autumn sunsets. "You can't eat sunsets" was his favorite expression. The old man had by now given up all hope of ever possessing Binya's umbrella. He wished he had never set eyes on it. Because of the umbrella, he had suffered the tortures of greed and the despair of loneliness. Because of the umbrella, people had stopped coming to his shop.

Ever since it had become known that Ram Bharosa had tried to have the umbrella stolen, the village people had turned against him. They stopped trusting the old man, and instead of buying their soap and tea and matches from his shop, they preferred to walk an extra mile to the shops near the Tehri bus stand. Who would have dealings with a man who had sold his soul for an umbrella? The children taunted him, twisting his name around. From "Ram the Trustworthy" he became "Trusty Umbrella Thief."

The old man sat alone in his empty shop, listening to the eternal hissing of his kettle and wondering if anyone would ever again step in for a glass of tea. Ram Bharosa had lost his own appetite, and he ate and drank very little. There was no money coming in. He had his savings in a bank in Tehri, but it was a terrible thing to have to dip into them! To save money, he had dismissed the blundering Rajaram. So he was left without any company. The roof leaked, and the wind got in through the corrugated tin sheets, but Ram Bharosa didn't care.

Bijju and Binya passed his shop almost every day. Bijju went by with a loud but tuneless whistle. He was one of the world's whistlers; cares rested lightly on his shoulders. But, strangely enough, Binya crept quietly past the shop, looking the other way, almost as though she were in some way responsible for the misery of Ram Bharosa.

She kept reasoning with herself, telling herself that the umbrella was her very own and that she couldn't help it if others were jealous of it. But she couldn't help feeling that in a small way she was the cause of the sad look on Ram Bharosa's face ("His face is a yard long," said Bijju) and the ruinous condition of his shop. It was all due to his own greed, no doubt. But she didn't want him to feel too bad about what he'd done because it made her feel bad about herself. So she closed the umbrella whenever she came near the shop, opening it again only when she was out of sight.

One day toward the end of October, when she had ten paise in her pocket, Binya entered the shop and asked the old man for a toffee.

She was Ram Bharosa's first customer in almost two weeks. He looked suspiciously at the girl. Had she come to taunt him, to flaunt the umbrella in his face? She had placed her coin on the counter. Perhaps it was a bad coin. Ram Bharosa picked it up and bit it; he held it up to the light; he rang it on the ground. It was a good coin. He gave Binya the toffee.

Binya had already left the shop when Ram Bharosa saw the closed umbrella lying on the counter. There it was, the blue umbrella he had always wanted, within his grasp at last! He had only to hide it at the back of his shop, and no one would know

that he had it; no one could prove that Binya had left it behind.

He stretched out his trembling, bony hand and took the umbrella by the handle. He pressed it open. He stood beneath it in the dark shadows of his shop, where no sun or rain could ever touch it.

"But I'm never in the sun or in the rain," he said aloud. "Of what use is an umbrella to me?"

He hurried outside and ran after her.

He wasn't used to running, but he caught up with Binya and held out the umbrella, saying, "You forgot it—the umbrella!"

But Binya didn't take the umbrella. She shook her head and said, "You keep it. I don't need it anymore."

"But it's such a pretty umbrella!" protested Ram Bharosa. "It's the best umbrella in the village."

"I know," said Binya.

She left the old man holding the umbrella and went tripping down the road, with nothing between her and the bright blue sky.

□ CHAPTER TEN □

Well, now that Ram Bharosa has the blue umbrella—a gift from Binya, as he tells everyone—he is sometimes persuaded to go out into the sun or the rain, and as a result he looks much healthier. Sometimes he uses the umbrella to chase away pigs or goats. It is always left open outside the shop, and anyone who wants to borrow it may do so. In a way it has become everyone's umbrella. It is faded and patchy, but it is still the best umbrella in the village.

People are visiting Ram Bharosa's shop again. Whenever Bijju or Binya stop for a cup of tea, he gives them a little extra milk or sugar. They like their tea sweet and milky.

A few nights ago, a bear visited Ram Bharosa's shop. There had been snow on the higher ranges of the Himalayas, and the bear had been finding it difficult to obtain food; so he came lower down to see what he could pick up near the village. That night the bear scrambled onto the tin roof of Ram Bharosa's shop and made off with a huge pumpkin, which had been ripening there. But in climbing off the roof, the bear had lost a claw.

Next morning Ram Bharosa found the claw just outside the door of his shop. He picked it up and put it in his pocket. A bear's claw was a lucky find.

A day later, when he went into the market town, he took the claw with him and left it with a silversmith, giving the crafts-man certain instructions.

The silversmith made a pendant for the claw, then he gave it a thin silver chain. When Ram Bharosa came again, he paid the silversmith ten rupees for his work.

The days were growing shorter, and Binya had to be home a little earlier every evening. There was said to be a hungry leopard at large, and she couldn't leave the cows out after dark.

She was hurrying past Ram Bharosa's shop when the old man called out to her.

"Binya, spare a minute! I want to show you something."

Binya stepped into the shop.

"What do you think of it?" asked Ram Bharosa, showing her the silver pendant with the claw.

"It's so beautiful," said Binya, just touch-ing the claw and the silver chain.

"It's a bear's claw," said Ram Bharosa. "I found it beneath the big oak tree. That's even luckier than a leopard's claw. Would you like to have it?"

"I have no money," said Binya.

"That doesn't matter. You gave me the umbrella—I give you the claw! Come, let's see how it looks on you."

He placed the pendant on Binya, and indeed it looked very beautiful.

She was halfway home when she realized she had left the cows behind.

"Neelu, Neelu!" she called. "Oh, Gori!"

There was a faint tinkle of bells as the cows came slowly down the mountain path.

In the distance she could hear her mother and Bijju calling for her.

She began to sing. They heard her singing and knew she was safe and near.

Binya walked home through the darkening glade, singing of the stars. The trees stood still and listened to her, and the mountains were glad.

RUSKIN BOND has lived in India for most of his life and currently makes his home some 7,500 feet up in the Himalayan foothills. He has written numerous books for children and adults, including *Grandfather's Private Zoo, Tales Told at Twilight,* and *The Hidden Pool.* Mr. Bond was a winner of the annual John Llewellyn Rhys Memorial Prize for outstanding first novel published in England.

VERA ROSENBERRY has illustrated many books for children, including *Savitri: A Tale of Ancient India* by Aaron Shepard and *Favorite Fairy Tales Told in India* by Virginia Haviland. Ms. Rosenberry lives on Long Island with her husband, who grew up in India. They have two grown children.